Catch me!

A TEMPLAR BOOK

First published in the UK in 2012 by Templar Publishing,
an imprint of The Templar Company Limited,
The Granary, North Street, Dorking, Surrey, RH4 1DN, UK
www.templarco.co.uk

Copyright © 2012 by Yokococo

First edition

All rights reserved

ISBN 978-1-84877-213-7

Edited by Hannah Wilson

Printed in Singapore

Yokococo

Hans and Matilda

templar publishing
www.templarco.co.uk

There was once a little cat
called Matilda.

And there was once a little cat called Hans.

They were SO different!

Everyone said Matilda was such a **good** girl.

But people said, "Be quiet, Hans!"

Everyone said Matilda was such a **sweet** girl.

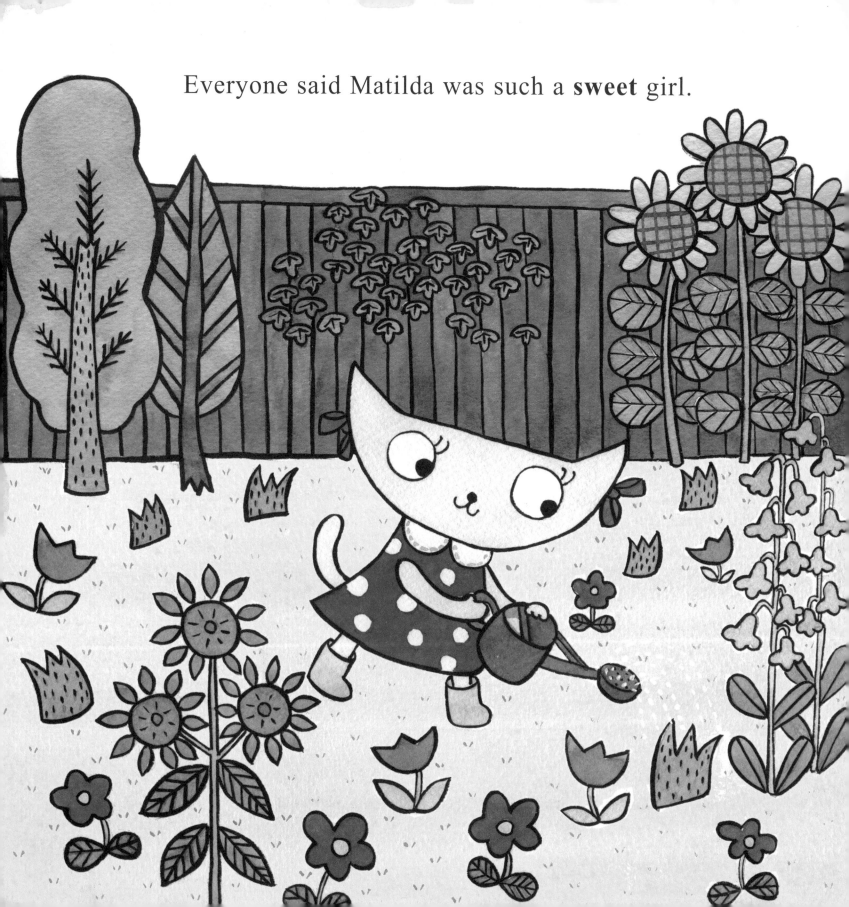

But people said,

"Stop it, Hans!"

Everyone said

Matilda was such a **thoughtful** girl.

But people said,

"Hans! How dare you!"

One night Hans went too far...

and climbed the gates of the zoo.

Hans borrowed a set of keys…

and set

all of the animals free!

"Oh dear!" said Matilda. "Naughty Hans!"

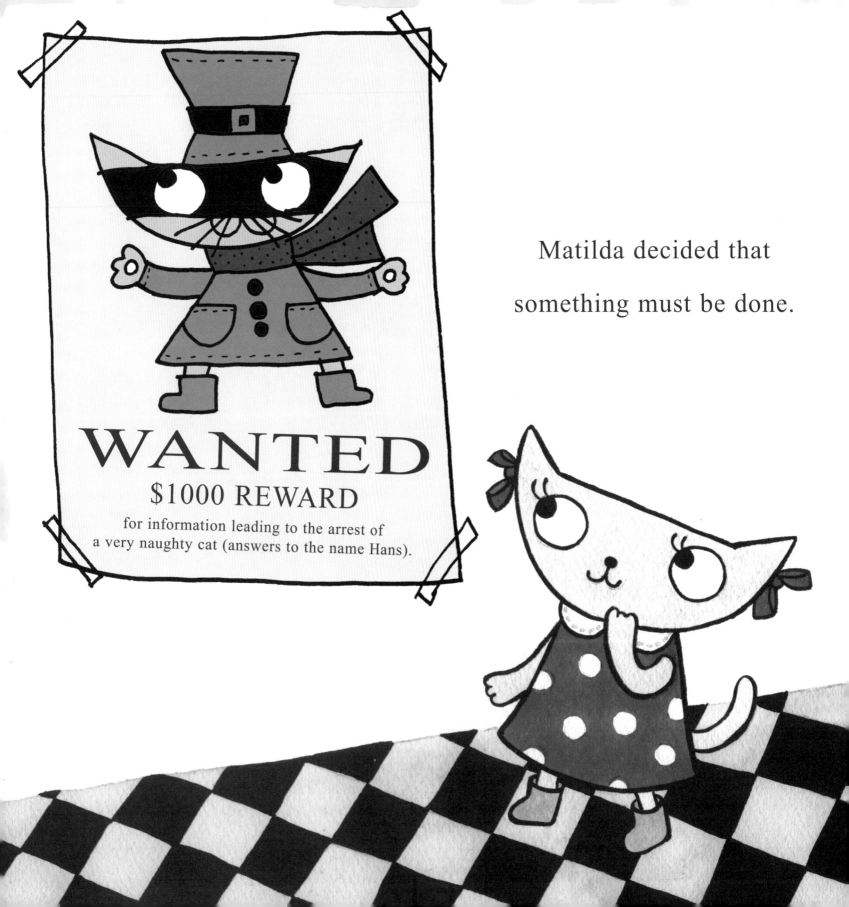

WANTED

$1000 REWARD

for information leading to the arrest of
a very naughty cat (answers to the name Hans).

Matilda decided that
something must be done.

"Excuse me," said Matilda.
"I know where Hans will be
at midnight tonight!"

"Thank you very much
for your information, Matilda,"
said the policeman.

On the stroke of midnight,

Hans was caught red-handed:

"Got you!"

shouted the policeman.

The policeman

took off

Hans's hat.

The policeman

took off

Hans's mask.

Finally, the policeman removed

Hans's whiskers.

And, underneath them he found…

"Can I have my reward now please,

Mr. Policeman?"

said Matilda

in a **very** sweet voice.

And she promised to be

very, very good from then on

(unless, of course, she was wearing a hat,

and a mask, and some whiskers).